TIMMY'S GIFT
A Christmas Story

Created by Samuel J. Butcher

A GOLDEN BOOK • NEW YORK
Western Publishing Company, Inc., Racine, Wisconsin 53404

It has been said that life is made up
of moments, and most certainly it is.
There are precious moments in time
when great deeds, both large and
small, are accomplished by an
ordinary someone, just like you and
me. This is a story of one of those
times when someone was called upon
to accomplish a very important task.
Let's start at the beginning on a very
special day many, many years ago.
A day when a heavenly light shone
down upon the earth and all the
angels rejoiced . . .

"My, oh, my!" said Angie. "I've never seen anything like it. Have you, Harold?"

"Not in a million years!" answered the little redheaded angel.

He turned to his friend Simon. "What does it mean?" Harold asked.

"Maybe Baruch will know," Angie said.

"Yes," Simon agreed. "Let's ask Baruch . . ."

The three little angels flew off to find their friend. As they headed toward the mysterious light, they peeked through the beautiful clouds in search of Baruch. At last, they found him studying in his library.

"Baruch," called Simon. "What is the light?"

The little scholar looked up. "The light?" he asked.

Angie nodded her head. "Yes. What does it mean? Tell us, please."

"Oh, the STARLIGHT!" Baruch smiled. "Yes! Isn't it magnificent? It comes from a special star which has been made to shine down upon the earth. But wait," he said, looking up. "Timotheus, please come down. You'll want to hear this, too."

Timmy was a tiny angel, much younger than the others. He was sitting on the library roof making cloud puffs when he heard Baruch's voice. Timmy straightened his halo and grabbed his tattered old blanket, which never left his side. He slid off the roof . . .

. . . and landed with a PLOP in the clouds below.

"What will I want to hear, Baruch?" asked Timmy.

"This light shining down upon the earth," Baruch explained while pointing to the Starlight, "leads to the place where a little Prince will soon be born."

"How wonderful!" said Harold. "Let us rejoice!"
"A baby Prince?" asked Timmy. "Really?"
"Yes," Baruch nodded. "He will be born into a family with no riches at all. But he *will* have a crown.

"It has been ordained," Baruch continued, "that one of us must journey to the earth and give this gift to the Prince."

"Oh, my!" said Angie. "Who will be given such a great honor?"

Baruch slowly showed the crown to each angel. When it reached Timmy, the crown began to glow brightly.

"As you can see, dear friends, the choice has been made."
Timmy looked at Baruch with wide eyes.

"I think the choice is great!" said Simon. "Unusual . . . but great."

Timmy shook his head. "There must be a mistake," he said, clutching his blanket. "I'm too little. And, besides, I'm always losing things."

"Yes, Timmy," Baruch agreed. "You do seem to lose everything. Everything but that," he said, pointing to the tattered blanket. "Won't it be difficult to carry that and the crown?"

Timmy hugged his blanket protectively. "It won't be any trouble at all."

"Then you can leave at once," Baruch said.

As he slipped through the clouds, Timmy heard Baruch say, "By carrying out this mission, you will learn why you have been chosen. Have faith, Timotheus, and remember to follow the Starlight."

With this great and noble
task before him, where would
Timmy begin his journey?

In the humble home of Nicodemus the Pig. KERPLOP!!! Timmy landed right in the middle of a pigpen.

"Are you all right?" asked Nicodemus.

"I think so," said Timmy.

"Very good." The pig snorted. "I'm sorry you dropped in when my house is such a mess." He giggled. "But then it's *always* a mess!"

Nicodemus tried to tidy up by patting his mud floor down flat. "I never have visitors," he said. "So I'm truly delighted to see you. I'm Nicodemus. What's your name?"

"My name is Timmy," said the little angel. "I'm following the Starlight on a very important journey. It's my job to deliver this beautiful crown to the little Prince who is to be born." He looked at the crown and himself—both were covered with mud. "Oh, my," said Timmy. "Angels aren't supposed to be dirty. Would you like to help me wash?"

"Wash?" asked Nicodemus. "What's *wash*?"

Timmy smiled and led Nicodemus to a nearby pond. He washed himself, the crown, his blanket, and the pig.

"There!" said Timmy. "Everything always looks better when it's clean. Why, Nicodemus! You're handsome!"

Nicodemus looked himself over and smiled. "My goodness, you're right!" he said. "Nobody else ever took the time to see who I really was under all that mud. Imagine you doing such a thing!"

Just then the Starlight moved across the sky.

"That light!" gasped Nicodemus. "Timmy, is that your star?"

The little angel grabbed his blanket and crown. "Yes!" he
said. "I have to go. I don't want to lose it."

Nicodemus waved good-bye. "I'd love to go with you, but
I've got *so* much work to do now. My house looks like a
PIGPEN!"

Timmy waved to the pig and ran after the Starlight.

Timmy hurried on, following the special light and leaving a happy . . . and very clean . . . Nicodemus behind. Even as the sky turned darker, and even as the wind blew cold and strong, the Starlight shone brightly.

All of a sudden the Starlight stopped moving. It was shining on a spooky old tree. Timmy looked up at the scary branches as they moved in the wind. He hugged his blanket close.

"Oh," he said, "I'm sure the bright light will start moving away from here any second . . . I hope."

Timmy tried to be brave. If the Starlight wouldn't move, it must mean that Timmy was needed here. So he took a few steps closer.

"There's nothing to be afraid of, anyway. It's just an old dead tree."

"AWAY!" yelled the terrible tree. "Go away and leave my forest! Run, I say! Begone."

"I . . . I want to," said a very scared Timmy. "But I can't!"

"Why not?" the tree roared.

"Because I'm supposed to follow the Starlight," Timmy answered. "And right now it's shining on you."

Timmy peeked into the tree's mouth. He saw a squirrel standing on a chair. He'd been yelling through the tree hole to make his voice sound bigger!

"Hey!" said Timmy, startling the squirrel.

"EEEEK!" yelled the squirrel in his loudest voice.

Timmy screamed and ran away from the tree. He dived into some bushes to hide.

"I must be brave," thought Timmy as he pulled himself up.

Timmy slowly peeked out of the bushes. "Well, what do
you know?" he said. "It *is* just a squirrel! Why were you
trying to scare me?" he asked. "I wasn't going to bother you."

The squirrel frowned at Timmy. "Oh, you weren't, were
you? And how was I supposed to know that? All the nuts I
gathered for the winter are stored in this tree. The last thing
I need is for a stranger to sneak up and rob me."

"I wasn't sneaking," said Timmy. "And I would never
rob anybody."

"Fine!" said the squirrel. "Then you can just go away. My nut supply is for me alone!"

A cold wind blew and made Timmy shiver.

"Oh, all right!" said the cranky little squirrel. "I guess you can come in. You might as well get warm and have some nuts. By the way, my name is Titus." And with that he stomped into his house.

Though he had precious little time, Timmy accepted Titus's invitation. Surely the Starlight had stopped there for some reason.

Inside the cozy little tree, Timmy and Titus warmed themselves by the fire.

"The filberts are tasty this year," said the squirrel. "But I recommend the walnuts."

Timmy waited politely until Titus handed him a bowl of nuts.

"Well, go on, try some," the squirrel said. "And if you're sleepy, there's an extra bed in the corner."

"Thanks," said Timmy. "But I have to go. I must bring this crown to the little Prince."

"Oh, well," the squirrel grumbled. "If you did stay the night, you'd probably steal my bed, too. But that would only serve me right for trusting strangers. I'm just a bushy-tailed fool."

Timmy shook his head. "No, you're not. You're kind and you're generous."

Titus was very surprised. He smiled a tiny smile. "Gee, thanks," he whispered. "But don't spread it around. I have my reputation to protect."

Just then the Starlight moved away from the tree.
"I've got to go," said Timmy. He bundled up the crown
and hurried out of the tree. "Thanks again for everything."

Titus waved to Timmy. "I'd like to see the little Prince," he said. "But I've got work to do here. I'm going to share my nuts . . . just a few, you understand . . . with all of the hungry forest animals! Bye, little angel."

With the squirrel's gentle farewell, Timmy set out once again to follow the Starlight.

The night grew windy and cold. The cold brought with it snow, and as the storm worsened, Timmy lost sight of the Starlight.

The wind blew sharply and made scary echoes. Timmy hugged his blanket. He was really frightened and tired now. So much so that he lost his balance and dropped the crown. He tried to pick it up, but it seemed to hop away. He grabbed the crown just as it began to move again. When he picked it up, what do you think he found?

A scared baby bunny was shivering in the snow.

"Don't cry, little bunny," said Timmy. "I won't hurt you."

"Are you a wolf?" asked the bunny.

"A wolf!" Timmy said with a laugh. "No! I'm an angel. See my halo and wings?" He pushed up his halo and smiled. "My name is Timotheus, but you can call me Timmy. What's your name?"

"My name is Snowflake," said the bunny.

The two new friends started off into the forest together.
"You don't have to be afraid, Snowflake," said Timmy.
"Then *you're* not frightened?" she asked. "Not even of
wolves?"

Timmy shook his head. "I have more important things to
worry about," he said, hugging his blanket. "I lost the
Starlight."

Snowflake looked up to the treetops. "But you can't *ever*
see starlight when you're this deep in the forest. You have
to get away from all these trees so you can see the whole
big sky."

Timmy sighed. "That's what I've been trying to do, but I don't know the way."

"The way to what?" asked Snowflake.

"The Prince," said the little angel. "I have to take this crown to the Prince."

Snowflake hopped ahead. "I can show you the way out of the forest," she said. "Let's go. Come on!"

Unbeknownst to Timmy and his new friend, they were
being watched and followed.

Timmy and Snowflake walked a long way through the
forest. The little angel held his blanket and the crown close
to him to keep them safe. When they reached the edge of the
forest, Snowflake and Timmy ran out into the open land and
heard a strange noise.

Still unaware that they were not alone, they stopped to listen.

"What could it be?" wondered Snowflake.

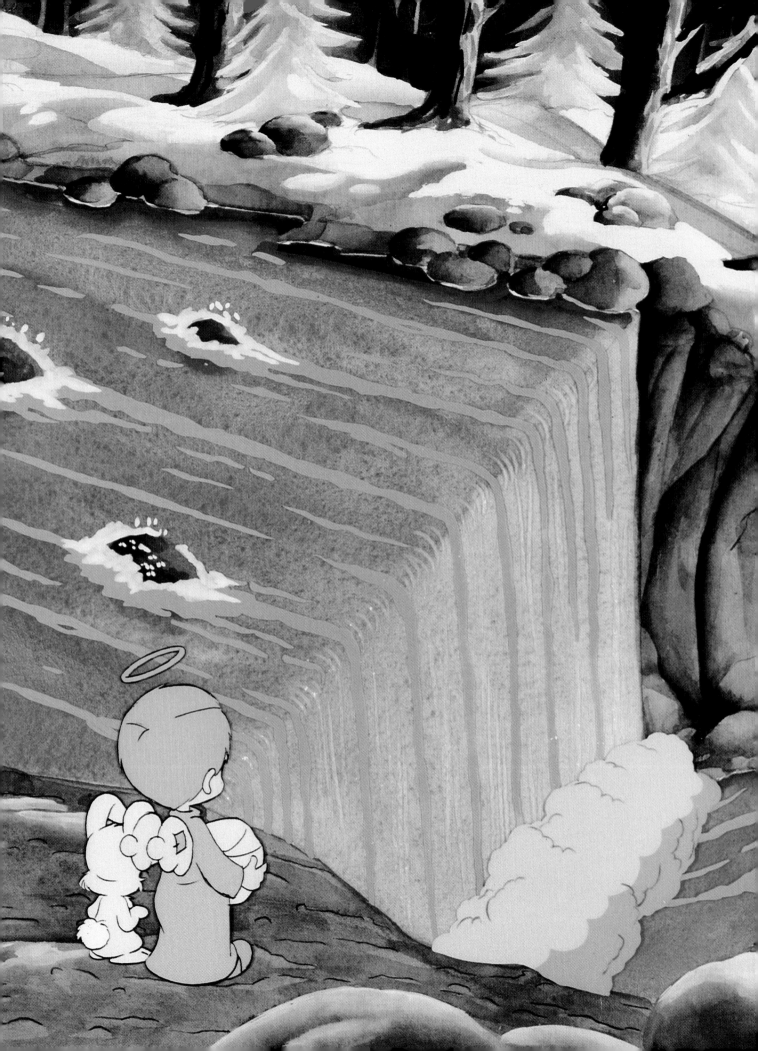

They soon came to a rushing river, with a thundering waterfall, that cut the land in two. They couldn't go any farther.

"Gosh!" said Timmy. "What do we do now?"

"Look!" the little bunny said, pointing to a dead tree. "There's a bridge." She giggled and scampered onto the fallen tree. Snowflake ran back to Timmy. "It's easy, see?" she said. "Want to try?"

Timmy thought it was probably easy for the bunny, but he wasn't too sure how easy it would be for him. He carefully stepped onto the tree, which began to quiver and creak. But he took a deep breath and put one foot in front of the other.

"That's the way," called Snowflake, who was waiting her turn. "You can do it. Keep going."

Even though the tree groaned under Timmy's weight, he turned to reassure the bunny.

When Timmy looked up, he saw the shadow of a fierce animal. It was about to pounce on Snowflake.

"SNOWFLAKE!" he shouted. "Look out! It's a W-W-W-WOLF!"

All at once the wolf, who had been stalking them, leapt
out of the bushes. He sailed right over Snowflake's head and
landed in a snowbank. But as the big ferocious wolf climbed
out of the snow, Timmy saw that he was really just a wolf cub
who had been practicing his stalking skills.

The cub stumbled clumsily over his too-big puppylike paws and tumbled toward the tree. When he jumped on it, the tree began to shift.

"No," called Timmy. "Go back. It's dangerous!"

But it was too late.

CRACK! The tree broke in half, and Timmy and the cub
fell into the river.

As Timmy splashed in the cold water, the current swept the crown away.

"The crown!" shouted Snowflake from the shore. "Get the crown!"

Still clutching his blanket, Timmy splashed after the crown.

Just then he heard the *very* scared wolf cub yelping and whimpering. Timmy glanced from the crown to the drowning cub. What could he do? He had to make a choice!

Without another thought, he threw out his blanket to the baby wolf. Timmy pulled and struggled against the current. They finally made it to shore just as the crown went over the waterfall.

Timmy did what he had to do . . . he had saved the cub, but the crown was now gone forever. Timmy's mission had failed.

The wolf cub shook himself off and ran to the trees. But before he disappeared into the forest, he turned to smile and bark a thank-you to Timmy.

Timmy dragged his wet blanket onto the bank and collapsed onto a tree stump. Tears began to trickle down the little angel's cheeks and onto his blanket.

"Don't cry, Timmy," said Snowflake.

"But I've lost the crown," cried Timmy. "And now I have nothing to give the Prince."

"You must go on, though," the little bunny said. "You've come such a long way. You can't give up now."

Slowly and sadly, the two friends continued to follow the Starlight. It grew brighter and brighter. From the top of a hill, Timmy saw that the Starlight was shining on a little town. It was the town of Bethlehem.

The Starlight came to rest on a stable. Timmy and
Snowflake hurried toward it.

They peeked through the doors and saw a beautiful light
shining inside. They moved closer to get a better look.
They saw a wondrous scene.

Mary and Joseph smiled silently at their new baby in a
bed of hay. Shepherds watched adoringly as Mary picked up
the little Prince.

"Oh, he must be cold," the little angel whispered.
"He doesn't have a blanket."

Timmy looked at his blanket and then at the baby. He looked back at his precious blanket. "I sure will miss you," he whispered without hesitation.

The little angel quietly
stepped forward and held out
his beloved blanket to the
baby's mother.

Mary took Timmy's gift
and smiled. She wrapped the
little Prince in the blanket and
laid him back in the manger.

And so it was that little Timmy, in one Precious Moment, gave all he had to the newborn Prince. And by this simple act, his heart was filled with the light of the brightest star . . . the Star of Christmas.